P9-DNK-470

E
FRE

First published in Great Britain in 1999 by David and Charles Children's Books.
Winchester House, 259-269 Old Marylebone Road. London NW1 5XJ

2 4 6 8 10 9 7 5 3 1

Text copyright © Vivian French 1999
Illustrations copyright © Jan Lewis 1999

The rights of Vivian French and Jan Lewis to be identified as the
author and illustrator of this work have been asserted by them in
accordance with the Copyright, Designs and Patents Act 1988.

ISBN 1 86233 005 0

A CIP catalogue record for this title is available from the British Library.

Printed in Italy

Big Fat Hen
and the
Red Rooster

Vivian French · Jan Lewis

David&Charles
Children's Books

The sun was peeping into Big Fat Hen's henhouse.

"Cluck cluck cluck!" said Big Fat Hen.
"Where is Red Rooster? It's getting late!"
She hurried out of the henhouse.

"Red Rooster! Red Rooster! The sun is up already!"
Red Rooster scrambled up to the farmhouse roof.

"Cock-a-doodle-doo! Cock-a-doodle-doo! Cock-a-doodle-doo!"

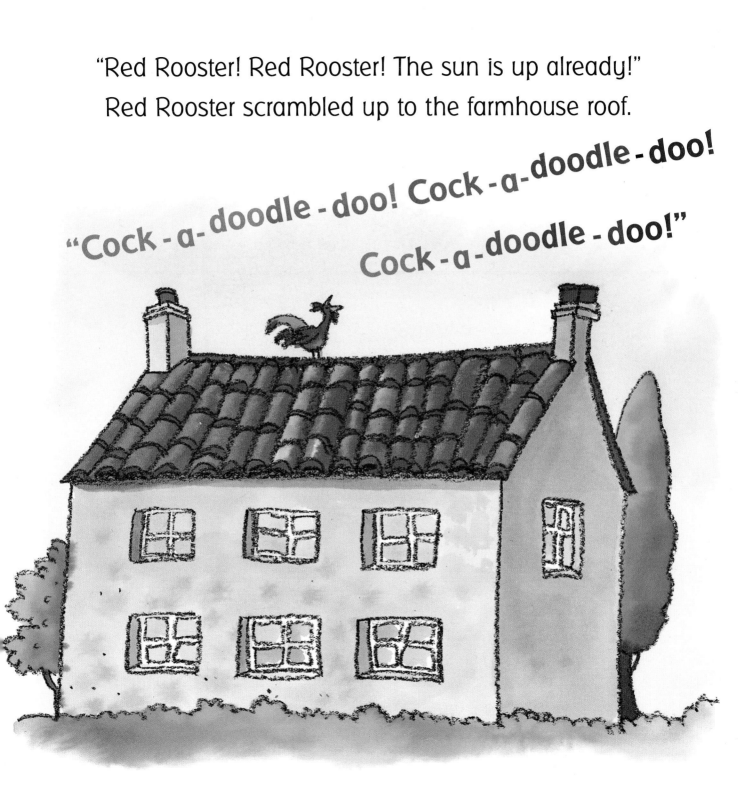

"OINK! Oink! Oink!"

Spotty Pig woke up from a dream
of delicious potato peelings.

"Moo! Moo! Moo!"

Brown Cow woke up from
a dream of sweet yellow hay.

"Baa! Baa! Baa!"

Woolly Sheep woke up from
a dream of fresh green grass.

"Dear me!
Time to get up!
Time to get to work!"

Farmer Tile jumped out of bed
and opened the farmhouse windows.

Red Rooster came
flapping down
from the roof.

"Thank you, Big Fat Hen," said Red Rooster. "It's hard
work waking up the farmyard every day."
Big Fat Hen fluffed out her feathers. "Don't
worry, Red Rooster. I will help you."
"Cock-a-doodle-doo!" said Red Rooster.

That night, Big Fat Hen went to bed early.
"Cluck cluck cluck!" she said to herself. "Tomorrow
I will wake up Spotty Pig and Brown Cow and Woolly
Sheep and Farmer Tile, and Red Rooster can sleep.
What a helpful Big Fat Hen I am!"

"Tu-whit, Tu-whoo!"

An owl flew over the farm.

"Cluck cluck cluck!"

Big Fat Hen woke up with a jump. "Is it morning?"
She hurried out of the henhouse and into the yard.
It was quite dark.

"Cluck cluck cluck," Big Fat Hen said to herself.
"It's not morning yet. But it will be soon."

Big Fat Hen bustled over to Spotty Pig.
"Cluck cluck cluck!" she said.
"Wake up, Spotty Pig!"

"Oink! Oink! Oink!" said Spotty Pig.
"It's MUCH too early. Go away, Big Fat Hen."

Spotty Pig went
back to sleep.

Big Fat Hen went back to the henhouse
and put her head under her wing.

"Squeak! Squeak! Squeak!"

A mouse rustled in the hay.

"Cluck cluck cluck!" Big Fat Hen woke up
with a jump. "It must be morning now!"

She hurried out of the henhouse and
into the yard. The moon was shining.
"Cluck cluck cluck," Big Fat Hen said to herself.
"It's not quite morning. But it will be very soon."

Big Fat Hen bustled over to Brown Cow.

"Cluck cluck cluck!" she said. "Wake up, Brown Cow!"

"Moo! Moo! Moo!" said Brown Cow.

"It's MUCH too early. Go away, Big Fat Hen."

Big Fat Hen went back to the
henhouse and put her head
under her wing.

"**Ark!** Ark! Ark!"
A fox barked in the field.

Big Fat Hen woke up with a jump.
"**Cluck cluck cluck!** I'm SURE it's morning now!"
She hurried out of the henhouse and into the yard.

"Cluck cluck cluck" Big Fat Hen said to herself. "It's not morning yet. But it will be very, very soon."

Big Fat Hen bustled over to Woolly Sheep.
"Cluck cluck cluck!" she said.
"Wake up, Woolly Sheep!"

"Baa! Baa! Baa!" said Woolly Sheep.
"It's MUCH too early. Go away, Big Fat Hen."

Big Fat Hen went back to the henhouse.
"It's very hard work being a helpful Big Fat Hen,"
she said to herself. She put her head under
her wing and went to sleep.

As the sun came up Farmer Tile stamped across the farmyard.

"What a noise!" she said. "All night long!
O**INK!** **Oink!** **Oink!** Moo! **Moo!** **MOO!**
Baa! **Baa!** **Baa!** I didn't get a wink of sleep!"
She rattled her buckets loudly and Red Rooster woke up.

"Cock-a-doodle-doo! Cock-a-doodle-doo! Cock-a-doodle-doo!" he crowed.

Spotty Pig, Brown Cow and Woolly Sheep woke up. "IT'S MUCH TOO EARLY, RED ROOSTER!" they all said together. "WE'RE SO TIRED!"

The sun peeped into the henhouse,
but Big Fat Hen did not wake up.

She was dreaming of
being a very helpful
Big Fat Hen!